To Jono, Jodi, Lily, and Oren
—J.J.

Dedicated to the baddest seeds I know:
Vincent and William
—P.O.

The Bad Seed
Text copyright © 2017 by Jory John
Illustrations copyright © 2017 by Pete Oswald
All rights reserved. Printed in the United States of America.
No part of this book may be used or reproduced in any manner whatsoever
without written permission except in the case of brief quotations
embodied in critical articles and reviews.
For information address HarperCollins Children's Books,
a division of HarperCollins Publishers, 195 Broadway, New York, NY 10007.
www.harpercollinschildrens.com
ISBN 978-0-06-246776-8 (trade bdg.)

The artist used scanned watercolor textures
and digital paint to create the illustrations for this book.
Typography by Jeanne L. Hogle
17 18 19 20 21 PC 10 9 8 7 6 5 4 3 2
❖
First Edition

THE BAD SEED

written by **JORY JOHN** • illustrations by **PETE OSWALD**

HARPER

An Imprint of HarperCollinsPublishers

I'm a bad seed.

A baaaaaaaaaad seed.

When they think I'm not listening, they mumble,

There goes a baaaad seed.

But I can hear them. I have good hearing for a seed.

Well . . .

I never put things back where they belong.

I'm late to everything.

I tell long jokes with no punch lines.

I never wash my hands.   Or my feet.

I lie about pointless stuff.

I cut in line. Every time.

I stare at everybody.
I glare at everybody.

I finish everybody's sentences. And I never listen.

And I do *lots* of other bad things, too.
Know why? Because I'm a bad seed.

A baaaaaaaaaaad seed.

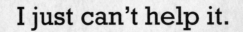

I just can't help it.

Sure, I wasn't *always* this bad.
I was born a humble seed, on a simple sunflower,
in an unremarkable field.

I had a big family.
Seeds everywhere.
We found ways of having fun.
We were close.

But then the petals dropped.

And our flower drooped.

It's kind of a blur.

fresh

SUNFLOWER SEEDS

DELICIOUS

I remember a bag. . . .

Everything went dark . . .

. . . and then . . . *then* . . .

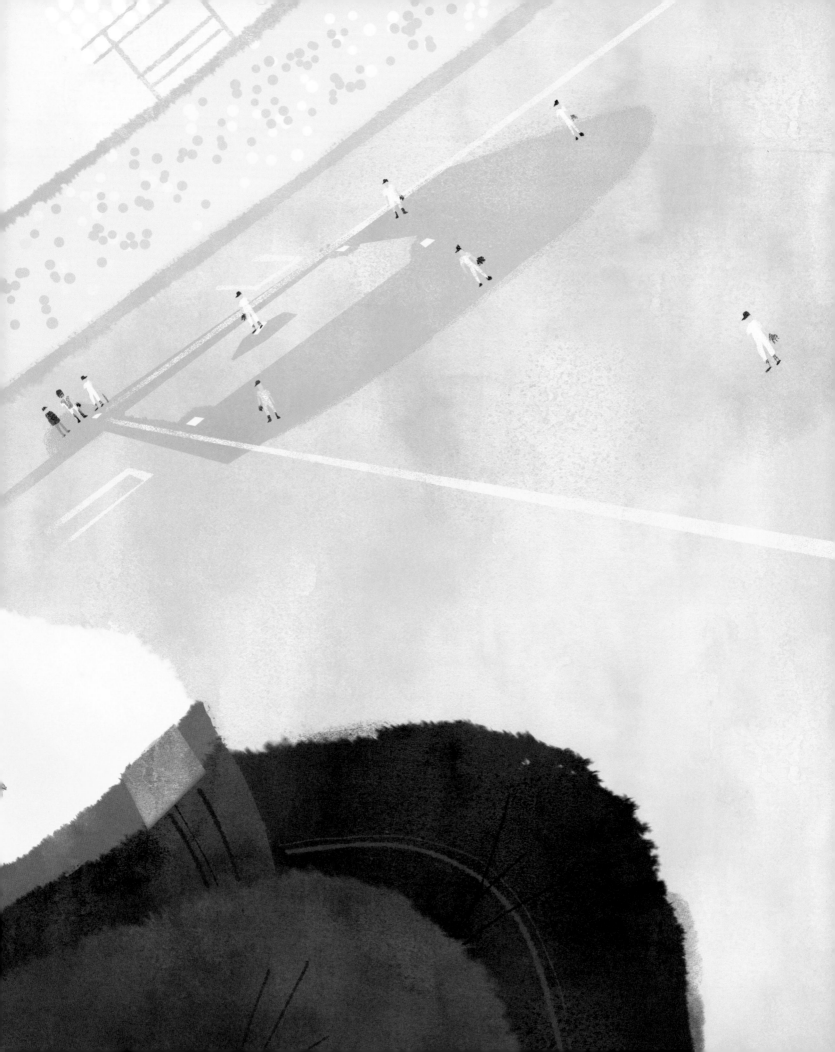

I thought I was a goner. . . .
I thought I was done for. . . .
I screamed and I hollered. . . .

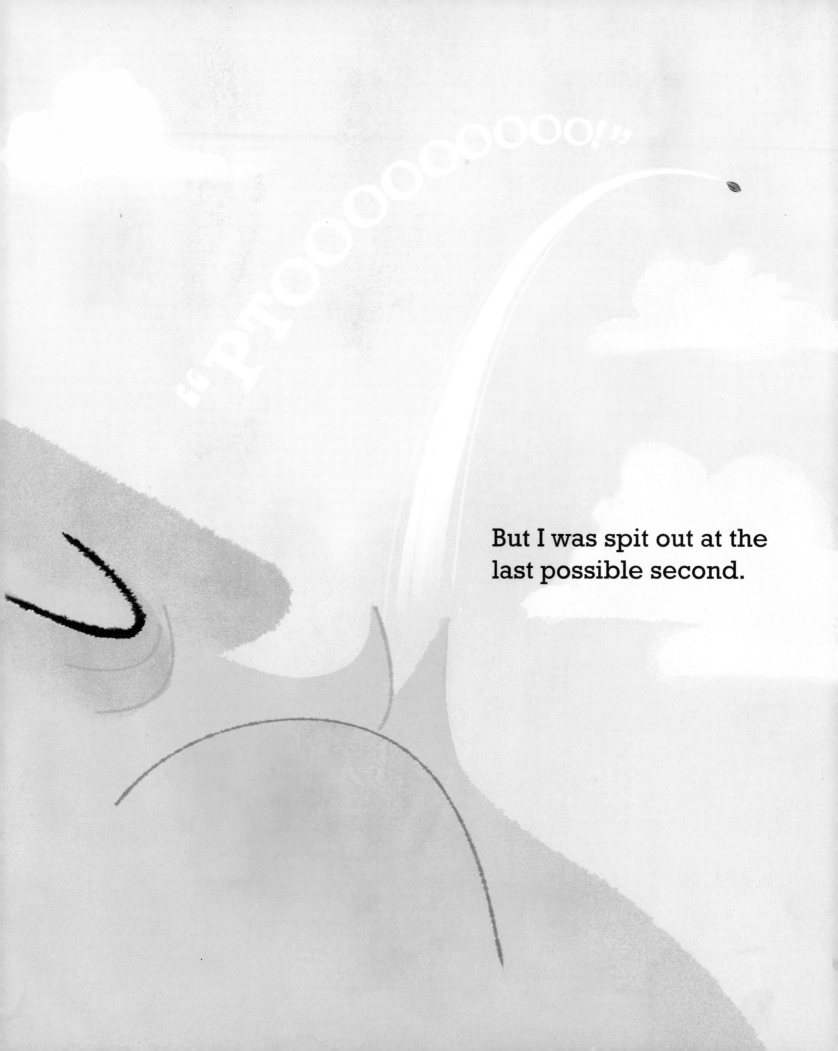

"PTOOOOOOOOOOO!"

But I was spit out at the last possible second.

I flew through the air, and I landed
under the bleachers with
a huge thud.

THUD!

When I woke up, it was dark outside.
A wad of gum had softened my fall.
I felt OK. But something had changed in me.
I'd become a different seed entirely.

I'd become a bad seed.

That's right.
I stopped smiling.
I kept to myself.
I drifted.

I was friend to nobody
and bad to everybody.
I was lost on purpose.
I lived inside a soda can.

I didn't care.
And it suited me.

Until recently.

I've made a big decision.
I've decided I don't want to be
a bad seed anymore.
I'm ready to be happy.

It's hard to be good when
you're so used to being bad.
But I'm trying.
I'm taking it one day at a time.

Sure, I still forget to listen.

And I still show up late.

And I still talk during movies. And I do all kinds of other bad stuff.

But I also say thank you.

And I say please. And I smile.

And I hold doors open for people.
Not always. But sometimes.

And even though I still feel bad, sometimes,
I also feel kind of good.
It's sort of a mix.

All I can do is keep trying.
And keep thinking,
Maybe I'm not such a bad seed after all.

I heard that.